Escape From Colditz

by

Deborah Chancellor

Illustrated by Phosphor Art

First published in 2007 in Great Britain by
Barrington Stoke Ltd
18 Walker Street, Edinburgh, EH3 7LP

www.barringtonstoke.co.uk

ISBN: 978-1-84299-454-2

Printed in Great Britain by Bell & Bain Ltd

For Harry, Edward and Imogen

Intro

The story you are about to read is true.

It is a tale of danger and courage in the dark days of World War II. On 21st September, 1941, two Dutch men escaped from the Colditz Prisoner of War camp in Germany.

Later they wrote down what happened, so this is how we know about their amazing wartime adventure ...

Cast List

Oscar Drijber
Conrad Giebel

Dutch officers who escaped from Colditz in August 1941

'Vandy'
(Machiel van den Heuvel)

Head of the Dutch Escape Committee

Officer Priem

Chief Security Officer at Colditz

'Max' and 'Moritz'

Dummies used to trick the German guards

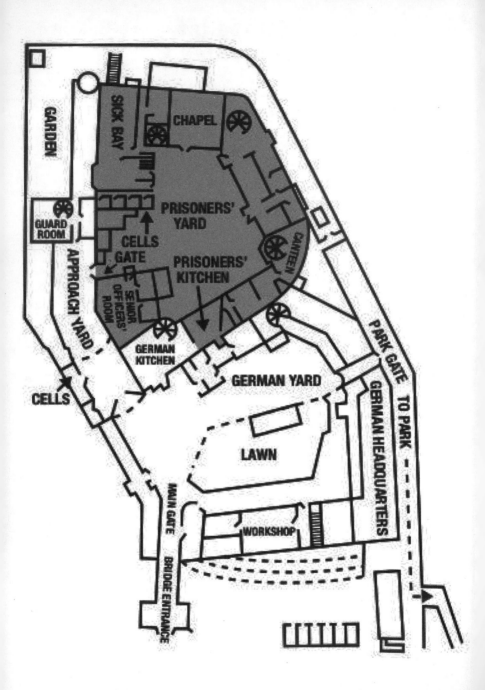

GARDEN

SICK BAY

CHAPEL

GUARD ROOM

PRISONERS' YARD

CELLS GATE

PRISONERS' KITCHEN

CANTEEN

APPROACH YARD

SENIOR OFFICERS' ROOM

CELLS

GERMAN KITCHEN

GERMAN YARD

PARK GATE

TO PARK

GERMAN HEADQUARTERS

LAWN

MAIN GATE

WORKSHOP

BRIDGE ENTRANCE

Contents

1   Colditz Castle   1

2   Preparations   7

3   The Chosen Two   13

4   False Start   18

5   Fixing The Count   24

6   Football Match   30

7   The Glass Bolt   35

8   On The Way   41

9   Light in the Dark   48

10   Home Run   58

Chapter 1
Colditz Castle

It is 1941. World War Two started two years ago. Deep in the middle of Germany, the Germans have turned an old castle into a maximum security Prisoner of War camp. This is Colditz Castle. In here, there are more German guards than prisoners. But all the prisoners believe it's their duty to escape. Their minds are made up. They must all get out, no matter how difficult it is.

The prisoners in Colditz are soldiers and airmen from many countries. They've come from places like Britain, France, Holland, Belgium and Poland. They're all in Colditz because they've tried to escape from other German prisons. The Germans are confident that none of them will escape from this fortress. Of course, the prisoners themselves have different ideas.

Inside the castle walls, the Prisoners of War meet together all the time to plan escapes. Groups from each country set up their own 'Escape Committees'. The different committees share their different information and skills. Who can pick locks? Who's good at making false identity papers and passports? The different Escape Committees help each other out. What the Germans have ended up doing is throwing together a bunch of escape artists.

One warm summer night in the middle of August, the Dutch Escape Committee has a noisy meeting. You can hear the sound of laughter from the Dutch block when you're outside in the prison courtyard. The German guards on duty look up and frown. They know only too well what the laughter is about.

"Congratulations, everyone!" shouts Vandy, the escape officer in charge of the meeting. "We did it!" He's grinning from ear to ear.

"Remember how our friends Hans and Francis escaped from Colditz last week?" he says. "We've just had news that they're out of Germany and in Switzerland! They did it! They're free now! It won't be long before they're back in Holland. Let's hear it for our heroes!"

The room bursts into cheers and yells of excitement. It's a few minutes before anyone can hear what else Vandy has to say.

"As you know, this is the first time any of us have made it out of Colditz to get all the way home. That means it's our first 'home run'. And it won't be our last."

Vandy's voice drops to a whisper.

"Our escape plan worked like a dream. Hans and Francis hid down that old well in the sports field outside the castle. Then they got over the wall at night, when no one was around. Their luck held, and now they're free."

A bold young officer puts his hand up. "Sir, I saw some guards at that well this afternoon. They screwed a bolt down onto the cover. You can't open the well now."

Everyone in the room turns to look at Vandy.

"That's right, Oscar," says Vandy. "Those goons – the Germans – have shut off our best escape route. Or that's what they like to think. I happen to disagree with them. I think we'll try and use that well a second time."

"But sir, what about the bolt on the cover?" asks Oscar. He looks puzzled.

"Do you think I haven't thought about that, boy?" replies Vandy. "Just listen to my plan."

Chapter 2
Preparations

The meeting of the Dutch Escape Committee goes on long into the night. By the time the last prisoner creeps back into his bunk, Vandy has a new escape plan ...

The next afternoon, there's prisoner exercise time as always. On the east side of the castle, there's an open field with barbed wire fences and tall stone walls all round it.

At 3pm, some guards take a group of prisoners down to the sports field. There are a few Dutch prisoners too. They have Bibles in their hands and look serious.

When the prisoners get to the field, the Dutch men move apart from the rest. They stand together in a small group. From a distance, it looks like they're saying their prayers. In fact, what they're doing is hiding Oscar in the middle of the group. And they're standing around the well. Oscar bends down to look at the bolt on the cover of the well. He measures it.

When they get back inside the castle, Oscar and his friends make a fake bolt that's just like the real one. The new bolt is made of a glass tube. The tube had aspirin pills in it before. But now it's empty and the prisoners paint it grey so it looks like it's made of iron, not glass.

"Just perfect," says Oscar as he looks at what the prisoners have done. "We'll take the real bolt off the cover of the well, then slot our fake one into place. When someone pushes up the cover from inside the well, *our* new glass bolt will shatter in a second."

Any escape will only work if every last detail is planned. Vandy knows that even if the escapers can break out of the castle, they'll need time to get as far away as they can before the guards sound the alarm. This means the Escape Committee will have to fix the prisoner head counts. That way the guards won't notice anyone's missing for a few days and the escapers can get far away.

As ever, Vandy has lots of ideas. He gives a workman at the castle a bribe and gets a sack of plaster. Then he asks a Dutch prisoner, who's a good artist, to make two

life-size dummies. In a few days, the artist has sculpted and painted the dummies. The men dress up the dummies to look like real Colditz prisoners.

Vandy is very happy. He asks a few men to come and look at the finished dummies.

"I've decided to call them Max and Moritz," Vandy says. "They'll come to roll call with us. When the German guards count the prisoners to see if everyone's there, they'll think the dummies are two real men. They won't notice anyone's gone missing."

One of the men at the meeting is an important army officer called Conrad. He's so impressed that he slaps Vandy on the back.

"Those dummies are great! They'll confuse the goons any day!" laughs Conrad. "But I hope I'm not still here to see it."

Suddenly Conrad's voice turns serious.

"Please pick me to make this escape, Vandy. I can't wait to get back to the army."

"We shall see, Conrad," replies Vandy. He knows it's time to choose the right men for the job. They need to get their full escape kit ready. They'll need good disguises, identity papers and plenty of German cash.

Who will Vandy choose? It won't be easy.

Chapter 3
The Chosen Two

Vandy thinks long and hard before he makes his choice. He'd love to escape himself, but he has made a promise. While he's the Dutch escape officer he won't break out of the prison. For now, he needs to stay inside Colditz and help others to get out.

In the last few days, Vandy has been watching Oscar. He thinks Oscar made a good job of the fake glass bolt for the well cover.

Oscar's a quick thinker and a hard worker, thinks Vandy, *plus he speaks good German and French. He has been on lots of holidays in the south of Germany, and knows the area very well. That could really come in useful.*

If the escapers manage to break out of Colditz, they will need to travel across the south of Germany to get to Switzerland.

Vandy has another good reason for wanting to choose Oscar. The young man is about to spend a fortnight in solitary confinement. That's a punishment. It means he'll be put in a prison cell all on his own because he tried to dig a tunnel out of Colditz. When the German guards caught Oscar and asked him about the tunnel, he didn't give away the names of any of his fellow escapers.

That man is loyal. We can trust him, thinks Vandy. *Perhaps this escape plan is something I can trust him with. As well as that, he deserves to miss those two weeks alone in a dark cell, with only the rats for company.*

Oscar is just 27 years old. He needs an older person to escape with. Someone who is wiser and who has more experience of life. Vandy thinks about choosing Conrad. This army officer is 41 years old. He's older than Oscar but still strong and physically fit. He really meant it when he said he wanted to get out and fight.

If Conrad does escape, Vandy thinks to himself, *he'll be very useful to the Dutch army – and after all, there is a war to be won outside these castle walls.*

Vandy has made his decision. Oscar and Conrad are the chosen, lucky pair. Vandy calls them both to a private meeting.

"You know what to do," says Vandy, when he tells Oscar and Conrad he's chosen them. "Keep this to yourselves. The fewer people we tell, the greater our chances of success."

Oscar and Conrad have a lot to do to get ready for their escape. They have to borrow some home-made clothes that are not army uniforms. Then they have to find fake passes and travel papers. Conrad has a secret supply of German banknotes.

"My wife sent me a food parcel from Holland," says Conrad. "She put this money inside." Conrad smiles. Perhaps it won't be too long before he sees his wife again.

Vandy asks a prisoner he knows well to make a compass. This will be a great help to Oscar and Conrad when they are travelling across Germany. Vandy also bribes a guard to give him a German newspaper. Oscar refuses to take the newspaper. In this time of war with Germany, he wants nothing to do with the German Nazis and their evil leader Adolf Hitler.

"You can carry that!" Oscar says to Conrad. "I'm not touching it!"

"Don't worry, I will," replies Conrad. "This newspaper will add the finishing touch to my disguise."

Everything's ready at last, and the two men are set to go.

Chapter 4
False Start

Vandy decides the best time to try and escape is on a Friday afternoon. The guards will be too busy thinking about the weekend. They won't be watching the prisoners properly. So, on the morning of Friday the 20th of September, Vandy sends a message to all the prisoners. Soon the prison is buzzing with gossip.

"Vandy wants us *all* to report for exercise this afternoon," one prisoner whispers to another. "He needs us to keep the goons busy. Something must be up. Let's go along and find out what."

All the prisoners in Colditz want to know what's going on. At 3pm, there's a crowd of men in the castle's inner courtyard. They all want to report for exercise. Normally about 80 prisoners go out to the sports field. Today there are over 200. This is far more than Vandy has expected.

The prisoners wait for the roll call. This is when the guards count them. It's like a prison register. The guards always do this before the walk to the field. Oscar and Conrad are waiting with everyone else. They are wearing their disguises under long army coats. Both feel sick with nerves.

The German Security Officer, Officer Priem, steps out in front of the crowd, and the prisoners fall silent. Priem waits for a moment before he speaks. He looks angry.

"There are too many of you here today for exercise to take place. I've cancelled today's walk to the sports field."

Things aren't looking good, but there's worse to come. Priem hasn't finished yet.

"All Dutch prisoners are banned from taking afternoon exercise until further notice. There will be no exceptions. Prisoners, you are dismissed."

As the crowd drifts away, Oscar and Conrad return to the Dutch block. They feel fed up and angry. Why has Officer Priem banned all the Dutch prisoners from exercise? Does he know about the Dutch escape plan?

That night, Vandy calls an emergency meeting of the Dutch Escape Committee. As he begins to talk, he's the only man with a smile on his face. For some reason, Vandy's still in a good mood.

"Cheer up, men!" he says. "Have you forgotten about the football match in the field tomorrow?" No one looks up, but he carries on.

"Remember, the Chief Commander of Colditz has planned a prisoner football competition for this weekend. He wants to keep us happy, to stop us trying to escape all the time. Just think. The competition can't happen if the Dutch team isn't allowed to play."

Vandy waits as the men take this in.

"My point is, Officer Priem can't carry out his threat to keep us all inside Colditz tomorrow. He won't dare go against his boss's wishes. If the Commander wants the football match to go ahead, it will."

Oscar smiles at Vandy.

"Of course! Holland versus Poland – that's the first match. I'd forgotten all about it."

Conrad isn't sure.

"Officer Priem meant what he said today," he says. "I'm telling you, Vandy, the Dutch are grounded."

Vandy steps forward and puts his hand on Conrad's shoulder.

"Don't give up, old chap," he says. "Let's see what tomorrow brings."

Chapter 5
Fixing The Count

The next day dawns. It's a bright, sunny September morning. As Oscar gets out of bed, he thinks, *Will this be the last morning I watch the sun rise from the other side of a dirty prison window?*

At breakfast in the canteen, the prisoners talk about the football competition. Many are upset that the Dutch team has been banned. "Why don't

we all stay away from the competition?"
one man says. "If the Dutch don't play, then
no one can play," he argues.

At that moment, the German Security
Officer walks into the canteen. Officer
Priem puts his hand up and the angry
prisoners fall silent. He looks embarrassed.

"The Chief Commander has asked me to
tell you today's football competition will
take place as planned. The Polish and Dutch
teams will both play. They can both take a
small number of men to cheer them on."

The prisoners cheer and whistle.

Priem goes on. "Do not think I have
gone back on my word." He looks a little
red in the face. "After the football is over,
the ban on Dutch exercise will come back
into force." Priem turns round and marches

out of the room. The prisoners' cheers turn into laughter.

"That will teach him a lesson!" grins Vandy. "I knew the Chief Commander would see things our way."

At 3pm that afternoon, the Polish and Dutch football teams meet in the inner courtyard. Among the Dutch supporters are Oscar and Conrad. This is the second day running they have come into the courtyard ready to escape. They're wearing their escape disguises under their coats again.

On every outing to the sports field, there are four head counts – one in the courtyard, two more in the field, and one last one when the prisoners come back to the castle. If things go well today, Oscar and Conrad will be missing on the way back. But the prisoners have a plan to cover this up.

Something's going on in the Dutch group. Two of the smallest men climb onto the backs of the two tallest men. It's as if they're getting a piggy-back ride. They hide under the tall men's coats. These two hidden men will stand in for Oscar and Conrad on the way back to the castle. The head count will be the same and the Germans won't see two men are missing.

Officer Priem arrives, and the first prisoner head count begins.

"... 63, 64, 65," counts a guard. Officer Priem jots down the total in his notebook. Another guard unlocks the gate that goes into the outer courtyard. The prisoners walk across this courtyard, then out under an archway. They walk down a path by the side of the castle down to the sports field. The guards don't see that the two tallest Dutchmen have very hunched backs.

67 prisoners make this journey to the field. With luck, two of them will never walk back up the hill to Colditz again.

Chapter 6
Football Match

The prisoners are in good spirits as they walk down to the sports field. They joke together about the football match. They try to predict the score. But Oscar and Conrad aren't thinking about football. Oscar feels inside his pocket for the glass bolt that he's hidden there. Soon it will be time to use it.

When the prisoners arrive at the grassy sports field, a guard blows his whistle. The men stand to attention for the second head count. Conrad looks quickly over at the two tall Dutch men who have the extra prisoners hidden under their coats. Their faces look blank. No one could guess there was anything odd going on.

"... 64, 65. Prisoners, stand at ease!" barks a German guard. As he turns to walk away, the two small men slip off the tall men's backs. They come out and walk around with the rest of the crowd. They do this with such speed and skill, the Germans don't see a thing.

The football match kicks off. Conrad, Oscar and a few others stand around the well, to one side of the pitch. Oscar bends down and tries to pull open the iron bolt, so that he can lift up the well cover. This is much harder than anyone expected. Oscar tries for a few minutes, then lets the other men have a go. They all try to shift the bolt, but it's stuck.

A whistle blows. For a moment, the men think it's time for the third prisoner head count. But no, it's half-time. They've almost forgotten that there's a football match going on ...

Oscar checks the score – it is Holland 3, Poland 1. That seems like a good sign. It makes him feel better. He tugs away at the bolt again. Suddenly, it moves a bit. Slowly Oscar pulls it back. He'll need the real iron bolt again later, so he slips it into his pocket. Then he hands the fake glass bolt over to his friends.

"Here we go, then," he says with a nervous smile.

Quickly, the men take off the well cover and put it down on the ground. There's not a moment to lose. Oscar climbs down into the well. Then Conrad follows him down. He stands on Oscar's shoulders. He leans

against the wall of the well, so that it will take some of his weight.

Both men look up as the well cover is put back. The bright blue circle of sky vanishes. Now they're in total darkness.

They listen as the fake glass bolt is put onto the cover. They can hear cheers – the football match must be over. The two men hear another whistle. This time it really *is* for the third head count.

"... 63, 64 ... 65. All present and correct!"

Oscar and Conrad have never been happier to hear the sound of a guard's voice. They hear boots shuffle above their heads. The prisoners are beginning their walk back to Colditz. Then there is silence.

Oscar and Conrad are on their own at last.

Chapter 7
The Glass Bolt

"Are you OK?" whispers Conrad.

"I don't think I can hold you up like this for much longer," replies Oscar. He shifts around in the dark. "If you climb down, there's just enough room for us both here."

A few moments later, the men are standing back-to-back in the narrow well, with little room to move. Conrad becomes anxious. He doesn't like being shut in.

"We can't wait until night time to get out of here," he says. "I think we should leave soon."

They wait for half an hour, then make their move. Conrad climbs back on Oscar's shoulders and pushes up the well cover. The glass bolt shatters easily and Conrad pulls himself out.

He runs across the empty football pitch, and heads for the trees on the other side of the field. Oscar has to scramble out of the well, tidy up the pieces of glass and put the iron bolt back on the cover of the well.

"Thanks for your help, sir," mutters Oscar as he races after Conrad.

Just beyond the trees is a barbed-wire fence. The two men climb over it slowly

and carefully. Then, they face another obstacle – the four-metre-high wall. Conrad goes first, and gets on Oscar's back to start climbing up the wall. Oscar's left on his own again. He has to claw his way up the brickwork. At the top of the wall are lots of bits of glass. Oscar only just misses cutting his hand on them. Then he jumps over the wall to the other side. He bumps into Conrad as he lands and almost knocks him over.

"Be careful," Conrad says. Oscar is annoyed.

"I'd like to see you get over that wall by yourself!" he snaps.

The two men are in a big vegetable garden. The sun is low in the sky, and the rows of neat plants cast long shadows as the light fades. But this is no time to admire the sunset. Oscar and Conrad creep through the garden and come to a road. To their horror, a German army officer rides past them on a bike. He doesn't stop, and this gives the men some hope. The alarm can't have been raised inside Colditz just yet.

Oscar and Conrad walk along the road and reach a crossroads. A sign points towards Leisnig, a town six miles away.

"That's the way to the station," says Conrad and sets off in that direction.

After a while, the two men pass some people on the footpath. Oscar remembers the correct greeting, *"Heil Hitler"*. The words almost stick in his throat but if he doesn't use them, the Germans may wonder why.

"*Heil Hitler!*" comes the reply. The Germans walk on. They carry on chatting to each other and ignore Oscar and Conrad. Oscar and Conrad start to walk more quickly. They both feel nervous.

It's dark when Oscar and Conrad get to the small town of Leisnig. At the railway station, Oscar buys their tickets.

"Two third-class tickets for Regensburg, please," he says and hands over the money.

A few people are waiting on the narrow platform for the next train. Oscar and Conrad step out into the moonlight to wait with them. Here they are, for all the world like two ordinary travellers. But, in fact, they're Prisoners of War on the run and only a few miles from Germany's most important prison camp. They're not ordinary travellers at all and the journey they have just begun is a dangerous one.

Chapter 8

On The Way

Oscar and Conrad are at the start of their journey across Germany. They'll be safe once they've got out of Germany and into Switzerland. Switzerland isn't in the war. There's no fighting there – and no German soldiers. They will take four different trains to get to the town of Singen, which is a few miles from the Swiss border. They get their first train now – the night express for Regensburg.

The steam train is almost full when Oscar and Conrad step on board. The lights are out in many of the carriages, because the passengers inside have already settled down for the night. Oscar and Conrad find a well-lit carriage and sit down next to two young women. A guard blows a whistle and the train pulls out of the station.

Thank goodness, the women soon get up and leave the carriage. Oscar and Conrad are left alone to try and get some sleep. Both men are totally worn out and need the rest.

Early the next morning, the train pulls in at Regensburg station. Oscar and Conrad get out to catch the connecting train to Munich. Before they know it, they're at Munich station, waiting for another train.

Munich is a big German city, and its main train station is a very busy place. The wide platforms are crowded with people. Oscar and Conrad are alarmed to see many men in the uniforms of the German army and air force. This isn't a safe place to stay for long.

The two men get on a train going to Ulm. They find two empty seats in a packed carriage. Conrad looks around at his fellow passengers. They seem friendly enough. He decides to try out some of his German.

"Would you like a cigarette, sir?" Conrad asks an old man, and he pulls a packet of English cigarettes out of his coat pocket. Someone in Colditz gave Conrad these cigarettes as a good-bye present.

Oscar's shocked. How can Conrad take such a big risk? Conrad talks with a strong

Dutch accent and everyone will look at his English cigarettes. It's impossible to buy English cigarettes in Germany. They haven't been on sale since the war began. Oscar gets up quickly from his seat and gives Conrad a sharp kick. He goes to the toilet and stays there for half an hour until the train arrives at Ulm station.

I'm not sitting next to that idiot, Oscar says to himself. *He'll give us both away in no time.*

Oscar and Conrad split up at Ulm station. They arrange to meet again on the next train to Singen and the Swiss border. As Oscar waits on the platform, a German officer in full Nazi uniform comes up to him.

"Why aren't you in the army, young man?" says the officer.

Oscar's heart skips a beat. This is the kind of question he's been dreading. He must give a good answer, or the worst could happen. If the officer suspects something, Oscar could be arrested and shot as a spy.

"There's been a mistake, sir," Oscar replies in his best German. "I didn't get my call-up papers in the town where I work. That's why I'm travelling to Singen. That's where my family live. I'm going to join the army there." The officer looks at Oscar, sniffs, and walks away. Oscar breathes a sigh of relief. The German has believed his story!

Exactly on time, the train for Singen arrives at the station. With shaking hands, Oscar opens a carriage door and climbs in. A few moments later, Conrad follows him in and sits down a few seats away.

As the train departs, the two men glance at each other. They don't need to speak. Both know how close they just came to disaster.

But things are looking up. They've travelled 700 miles across enemy territory, and now they're almost at the Swiss border.

Chapter 9
Light In The Dark

Oscar and Conrad look out of the window as the train pulls in at Singen station. This is the last stop on the line before the Swiss border. The platform is crowded with people. The Germans have set up an army checkpoint. They want to look at everyone's identity papers.

The two Dutchmen get out their fake passes ready for inspection. There are soldiers with guns everywhere. They're guarding every possible exit. Two senior officers are checking papers at a desk by the ticket office. And beside them are guards holding machine guns.

Oscar remembers the army officer back at Ulm station, and feels sick. If the guards at this checkpoint work out that their passes are fake, that will be the end of their freedom. At best, if Oscar and Conrad can get the soldiers to believe that they're Prisoners of War, they'll be sent back to Colditz. At worst, the soldiers will think they're spies, and shoot them dead on the spot.

Conrad looks at Oscar. He can see that the younger man's very nervous and scared.

"Keep calm, Oscar, we're almost there now. Show the soldiers your papers quickly, and don't look anyone in the eye. See you outside the station."

The two men separate and show their passes at the checkpoint. To their amazement, no one asks them any questions. They meet up again on the road that goes away from the station. The sun has set and it's getting dark.

As the men leave the town of Singen, the road takes them into a pine forest. They walk down a steep hill, and then up another. The men are tired. They mustn't waste energy by walking in the wrong direction. They know that the Swiss border is just two miles south-west of Singen. Oscar thinks they may have set off in the wrong direction.

"We need to check where we are," he says to Conrad. "Where's the compass? I think you had it."

Conrad looks awkward.

"I sat on it yesterday and broke it," he admits. "I had to throw the bits away."

Oscar is mad with anger, but this isn't a good time to start an argument. He gives a sigh and looks up at the sky. The first stars are beginning to twinkle.

"We'll just have to use the stars to work out which way to go," he says in a low voice. "That's the Pole Star, so that way must be North. We should go *this* way."

The two men set off towards the south-west. They leave the road and walk through the trees. After a while, they come to some open country. They cross some fields and find the railway line again. They follow the tracks and go past a road bridge. Then they slide on their stomachs down the slope to the railway tracks.

"Why can't we walk down the slope?" Conrad mutters. Just as he says this, a flashlight sweeps across in front of them. It just misses them! There's a German guard standing on the road bridge they've just passed.

"That's why!" hisses Oscar.

The two men cross the train tracks and go up the grassy bank on the other side. A road runs alongside the railway track. Oscar and Conrad are still lying on the ground, but they can see that this road leads to a checkpoint. They can see German soldiers standing by a wooden gate that blocks the road. The soldiers' machine

guns are glinting in the moonlight. This
must be the Swiss border control.

Across the road, there's another forest.
Oscar and Conrad could hide in the trees as
they make their way into Switzerland. The
only problem is, they'll have to cross the
road to get to the forest and the German
soldiers will see them and may shoot.

The moon is high and bright in the sky.
The two escapers wait for it to slip behind
a cloud. Two hours pass, the longest two
hours of their lives.

Suddenly, the moon vanishes. It's pitch
dark. Oscar and Conrad grab their chance
and run across the road. The German
patrol doesn't see them. Then they run
into the trees as fast as their legs will
carry them.

Now they're hidden in the forest, they keep running. They need to get as far away from the border checkpoint as they can, and as quickly as possible. Suddenly, they come onto another road.

"Stop!" a voice shouts.

Oscar takes a huge gamble and stops running.

"Don't shoot!" he calls out in French. He's sure that the voice in the dark belongs to a Swiss guard. "Show your face?" Oscar asks, again in French.

The guard shines a torch on his face. He's smiling.

"No German guard would dare do that. He'd make himself a target in the dark!" says Oscar. And he steps forward into the

torchlight. Tears of joy stream down
his face.

"Conrad, come here!" he calls out.
"We're safe. We're in Switzerland now!
There are no enemies here!"

Chapter 10
Home Run

Back in Colditz, Vandy's plan has worked like clockwork. The German guards still don't know that two prisoners have escaped. When the footballers come back from the field late on Saturday afternoon, the head count is the same as it was when they set out. No one suspects anything. 65 men are counted back inside the castle walls, just as the Germans expect.

For the next six roll calls, the prisoners use Max and Moritz, the plaster dummies. The dummies work so well that Vandy hides them away again before the guards find out what's going on.

"We'll use these two dummies again another time," he says. "Oscar and Conrad have been gone for 48 hours now. That's enough time to get well away from here."

The Germans find out that two prisoners have gone on the morning of September 23rd. By this time, Oscar and Conrad are waking up to freedom in Switzerland.

The Swiss let them stay in a hotel for a week. In the hotel Oscar and Conrad remember how hard life was at Colditz Castle. They write a letter in secret code to send to their friends still inside Colditz.

The letter tells the prisoners in Colditz about how they got out of Germany.

"Maybe this will help some more of our men to escape," says Oscar.

Oscar and Conrad want to do everything they can to help the prisoners of Colditz. They travel on to Geneva, the capital of Switzerland. They ask a skilful carpenter to make a special wooden chessboard. The chess pieces are all hollow. Oscar and Conrad fill them with German banknotes, maps, and other things which could help someone to escape. Then Oscar and Conrad wrap the chessboard up in a Dutch newspaper. The newspaper has a speech made by the Dutch Queen. Oscar and Conrad want this to give the men inside Colditz some hope.

This will cheer them all up! thinks Oscar as he wraps up the parcel, and posts it back to Colditz.

Both the chessboard and the newspaper make it all the way into the German Prisoner of War camp. Vandy's very happy to get them. He calls a meeting of the Dutch Escape Committee.

"We're here to celebrate another successful Dutch home run!" he tells his men. When the cheers die down, Vandy shows everyone the chessboard. They open it up. Everyone's impressed. The Escape Committee examines everything with great care.

"Good old Oscar and Conrad," says Vandy. "They deserve all the luck they get."

Then, in a solemn voice, Vandy reads out the royal message from the Dutch Queen, in the newspaper. There's a silence.

"We will take courage and hope from our Queen," says Vandy. "And above all, in the true spirit of Colditz, we will never give up."

Barrington Stoke would like to thank all its readers for commenting on the manuscript before publication and in particular:

Sarah-Frances Bateson
Charlotte Beare
Amber Brown
Lorraine Byles
Sophie Chapman
Alicia Cooper
Taylor Cooper
Jonathon Druce
Jake Fenton
Rebekah Gaskin
Mary Griffin
Daniel Griffiths
Daniel Guy

Philippa Heath
Emily Hentham
K Heywood
Luke Hirst
Megan Hopkins
June McCleave
Becky Pyke
Martin Slater
John Small
Nicolle Smith
Ben Welsh
Claire Whitehouse

Become a Consultant!

Would you like to give us feedback on our titles before they are published? Contact us at the e-mail address below – we'd love to hear from you!

info@barringtonstoke.co.uk
www.barringtonstoke.co.uk

AUTHOR CHECK LIST

Deborah Chancellor

What was the worst escape plan anyone ever tried to get out of Colditz?
One of the worst escape plans at Colditz very nearly worked. A French officer dressed up as a woman, and just walked out of the prison, through the gates! A prisoner shouted out after him when he dropped his watch on the ground. He didn't stop to pick it up, and that made one of the guards think there was something wrong.

What's your favourite fact about Colditz?
In 1941, a group of French prisoners spent nine months digging an escape tunnel that was so big, the prisoners called it the Métro. The Métro is what the underground is called in Paris. The amazing tunnel was 44 metres long. The German guards found out about it just a few metres before it was finished.

Who would you most like to be stuck in a prison cell with? And why?
I'd like to be with someone who was very good at escaping. Harry Houdini, the famous escape artist, would be good ...

Who's the last person you'd like to be stuck in a prison cell with? And why?
I'd hate to be in a prison cell with anyone who snores, or who tells long, boring stories.

If you had to use a false identity for a day, who would you be?
I'd like to pretend to be the head of MI5. I'd be able to look at all the MI5 files and find out some interesting top-secret information.